The Little Red Hen

A Viking Easy-to-Read Classic

retold by **Harriet Ziefert**

illustrated by **Emily Bolam**

VIKING

VIKING
Published by the Penguin Group
Penguin Books USA Inc., 375 Hudson Street, New York, New York 10014, U.S.A.
Penguin Books Ltd, 27 Wrights Lane, London W8 5TZ, England
Penguin Books Australia Ltd, Ringwood, Victoria, Australia
Penguin Books Canada Ltd, 10 Alcorn Avenue, Toronto, Ontario, Canada M4V 3B2
Penguin Books (N.Z.) Ltd, 182–190 Wairau Road, Auckland 10, New Zealand

Penguin Books Ltd, Registered Offices: Harmondsworth, Middlesex, England

First published in the United States of America by Viking,
a division of Penguin Books USA Inc., 1995

Published simultaneously in Puffin Books

1   3   5   7   9   10   8   6   4   2

LIBRARY OF CONGRESS CATALOGING-IN-PUBLICATION DATA
Ziefert, Harriet.
The little red hen / retold by Harriet Ziefert;
illustrated by Emily Bolam.   p.   cm.—(Viking easy-to-read classic. Level 2)
"Ages 5-8, beginning to read."
Summary: The classic tale of the hen who has no one to help her grow, harvest,
and mill the wheat, but several who want to eat the fruit of her labors.
ISBN 0-670-86050-6 (hardcover). — ISBN 0-14-037817-0 (pbk.)
[1. Folklore.] I. Bolam, Emily, ill. II. Title. III. Series.
PZ8.1.Z55Li 1995 398.2—dc20 [E]   95-11149 CIP AC

Printed in the United States of America   Set in New Century Schoolbook

Viking® and Easy-to-Read® are registered trademarks of Penguin Books USA Inc.

Reading level 1.9

The Little Red Hen

A little red hen
lived on a farm with

a dog,

a goose,

and a cat.

One day the little red hen
found some grains of wheat.

"Who will help me plant the wheat?"
asked the little red hen.

"Not I!" said the dog.
"Not I!" said the goose.
"Not I!" said the cat.

"Then I will plant it myself,"
said the little red hen.

And she did!

The little red hen watered
and weeded and watched.
She watched the wheat grow.

One day the wheat was ready to be cut.
"Who will help me cut the wheat?"
asked the little red hen.

"Not I!" said the dog.
"Not I!" said the goose.
"Not I!" said the cat.

"Then I will cut it myself,"
said the little red hen.

And she did!

"Who will help me beat the wheat?"
asked the little red hen.

"Not I!" said the dog.
"Not I!" said the goose.
"Not I!" said the cat.

"Then I will beat it myself,"
said the little red hen.

And she did!

"Who will help me take
the wheat to the mill?"
asked the little red hen.

"Not I!" said the dog.
"Not I!" said the goose.
"Not I!" said the cat.

"Then I will take it myself,"
said the little red hen.

And she did!

The little red hen
came back with flour.

"Who will help me
bake the bread?"
she asked.

"Not I!" said the dog.
"Not I!" said the goose.
"Not I!" said the cat.

"Then I will bake it myself,"
said the little red hen.

And she did!

The bread came out of the oven.
It smelled good. Very good.

The dog, the cat, and the goose
smelled the bread.
They ran to get some.

The little red hen put
the bread on the table.

"Who will help me eat
this good bread?"
asked the little red hen.

"I will," said the goose.

"I will," said the cat.

"I will," said the dog.

"Oh no, you won't!"
said the little red hen.

And she ate it all up herself.